	DATE DUE		

16869 HC

Peck Robert Newton

F

PEC   Soup's goat.

9.95

Feathers are flying and Soup fans will be cheering as Soup and Rob find themselves in the middle of their most riotous and chaotic adventure yet.

Oil and water don't mix—neither do ducks and goats. But for Soup, that's all the more reason to bring them together. It's the first annual goat race and Soup and Rob would like to win. The chances of that are pretty slim if they have to rely on an ornery goat and an old laundry basket to pull them across the finish line. Fortunately, they can always depend on Soup for that extra bit of scheming that's bound to put them in the lead. With a little help from squeaky-clean, dirty-mouthed cousin Sexton, sweet-talking Norma Jean Bissell and half of Arno Fletcher's barnyard, Soup hatches a plan that's sure to raise a ruckus, but just might mean victory, too.

Full of surprises and the usual Peck of trouble, *Soup's Goat* offers hilarious proof that life is not all work down on the farm.

SOUP'S GOAT

BOOKS BY ROBERT NEWTON PECK

A Day No Pigs Would Die
Path of Hunters
Millie's Boy
Soup
Fawn
Wild Cat
Bee Tree (poems)
Soup and Me
Hamilton
Hang for Treason
Rabbits and Redcoats
King of Kazoo (a musical)
Trig
Last Sunday
The King's Iron
Patooie
Soup for President
Eagle Fur

Trig Sees Red
Basket Case
Hub
Mr. Little
Clunie
Soup's Drum
Secrets of Successful Fiction
Trig Goes Ape
Soup on Wheels
Justice Lion
Kirk's Law
Trig or Treat
Banjo
Soup in the Saddle
Fiction Is Folks
The Seminole Seed
Duke
Soup's Goat

SOUP'S GOAT

Robert Newton Peck

ILLUSTRATED BY CHARLES ROBINSON

Alfred A. Knopf NEW YORK

THIS IS A BORZOI BOOK PUBLISHED BY ALFRED A. KNOPF, INC.

Text Copyright © 1984 by Robert Newton Peck
Illustrations Copyright © 1984 by Charles Robinson
All rights reserved under International
and Pan-American Copyright Conventions.
Published in the United States
by Alfred A. Knopf, Inc.,
New York, and simultaneously in
Canada by Random House of
Canada Limited, Toronto.
Distributed by Random House, Inc., New York.
Manufactured in the United States of America
1   2   3   4   5   6   7   8   9   10

Library of Congress Cataloging in Publication Data
Peck, Robert Newton.   Soup's goat.
Summary: Clean and tidy cousin Sexton
lends his unusual talent to Soup and Rob
as they engage in the town's goat-cart race.
[1. Country life—Fiction. 2. Vermont—Fiction]
I. Robinson, Charles, 1931-   ill. II. Title.
PZ7.P339Sob 1984   [Fic]   83-16245
ISBN 0-394-86322-4   ISBN 0-394-96322-9 (lib. bdg.)

SOUP'S GOAT

One

"Ready?" Soup asked me. "Let's go."

"No," said Mama. "Robert can't go to greet your out-of-town company until we brush his hair proper."

Soup, with his hand starting to rattle the latch of our kitchen door, made a wry face as he squinted at my hair. "So that's what that stuff is."

My mother ignored Soup's remark, but I saw Aunt Carrie give Soup a look of warning. "Now remember," Mama told me, giving my hair a few more swipes with a wet brush, "it's Sunday evening. So you're *not* to overstay your welcome past dark. Hear?"

"Yes'm," I said.

"Both of you have early chores and school tomorrow."

"I'll fetch myself home in good season," I told Mama. "I promise."

"He ought to wear a necktie," said Aunt Carrie.

I winced. So did Soup, who was already choking inside *his* tie. Then I saw a slight smile twitching his mouth; one that spelled joy for him, yet misery for me.

"I'm wearing mine," he said in his polite voice, which made me hope he'd hang in it.

There was no use, I knew, in fighting the torture. Mama roped me into my only tie, knotting it around my skinny neck until she was sure my face was purple and I wouldn't be able to breathe until bedtime.

My mother let out a long sigh. "There," she said, "I guess you're final decent."

"Let's go," Soup said again.

The two of us exploded out of the door, heedless of the flood of instructions that Mama and Aunt Carrie were offering with regard to appearances and conduct. Side by side, we started uproad to the next farm, where the Vinsons lived.

Soup, whose real name was Luther Wesley Vinson, was my closest pal. And I was also his. Soup was a year and four months older than I was; he could beat me up whenever he wanted to, so I usual allowed him to be the boss. There was no sense in becoming his enemy. Because being Soup's pal was trouble enough.

"It's only for two weeks," said Soup, kicking a pebble along the road.

"What is?"

Soup sighed. "My cousin's visit."

"How come he's going to stay at your house for two weeks? Doesn't he go to school up in Burlington?"

As we hiked along the dirt road, Soup sort of shook his head. "Nope," he said, "he goes to prison."

"*Prison?*"

"Yup. He goes to some religious school and it's already over for the year. Ma says he's a very proper kid. She also said that the pair of *us* could learn a lot from my cousin."

"About what?"

"Behavior." Picking up a stone, Soup chucked it at a willow tree that was still yellow with its fresh crop of May leaves. "According to Ma and Pa, this cousin of mine is half angel and half saint."

I threw a stone at the next tree. Soup and I had done so much throwing over the years, it was amazing that there was still so many stones along the road. Yet there always were. It sort of bugged me a bit to admit that Soup's stone always sailed farther than mine.

"I don't guess," I said to Soup, "that your cousin comes to visit you very often."

"Right. I once visited him and his folks, years back. As I recall, that one time was ample plenty."

"Maybe he'll be a lot of fun."

Soup made a sour face. "And maybe cows will fly."

"Your aunt and uncle will be coming too, won't they?" I asked.

Soup was busy juggling three pebbles into the air

and then dropped two of them. "They'll be coming. Then going. Good old Uncle Bunker and Aunt Louise never really approved of me. Not since I taught their perfect little precious how to deal from the bottom at poker. They caught us playing Spit in the Ocean."

Had I not been wearing a tie, I would have busted out a laugh. As we neared Soup's house, I asked him another question about his relatives. "Are their names Vinson, like yours?"

"Nope," said Soup. "Aunt Louise is Pa's sister. But her married name's Louise Dilly because that's her husband's name. Bunker Dilly."

"What's the kid's name?"

Soup shot me a grin. "You'll find out."

As I looked at the house where Soup lived, I pointed. "There's a car out front."

"Shucks," said Soup in a gray voice that seemed to be resigned to impending agony. "They're here."

People stood beside the car.

Less than two minutes later, I was introduced to Soup's relatives. I shook hands with Uncle Bunker, who patted me on the top of my head. I also met Aunt Louise, who sort of looked at me with her nose in the air, like she wanted to scrape me off her shoe. Last of all, I met their darling son.

"Boys," said Aunt Louise, in a voice she'd probable use to introduce a sultan or a king, "this is our little Sexton."

Sexton Dilly was short, skinny, and pale. He wore

glasses, which made him look like a bug that was pretending to be an owl. Some loving hand had parted his hair in the middle as though it had used an axe. The kid was wearing a dark-blue velvety suit. Beneath his chin was a red bow that was at least three sizes too fluffy for a Christmas wreath on a church door.

"Luther, you remember your cousin," Mrs. Vinson said to Soup. "Sexton will be with us for two whole weeks. Won't that be nice?"

"Peachy," said Soup.

"Come on inside," said Soup's pa. Then he looked at the three of us. "But, on second thought, I s'pose you youngsters hanker to stay outside and play."

Turning to Sexton, his mother bent forward with a quick warning. "Get dirty," she slowly whispered, "and I'll fry your fanny."

I pretended not to hear. Mr. and Mrs. Vinson took Aunt Louise and Uncle Bunker inside, which left Sexton Dilly in the company of Soup and me.

Soup scratched his head. "I reckon," he said to his cousin, "that by this time you probable forgot how to play Spit in the Ocean."

Sexton nodded.

"Can ya play baseball?" I asked Sexton.

"No."

"How about football?"

"No thanks."

"Well," said Soup, "maybe the three of us could dig

up some worms and go fishing? Would ya like to do that, Sexton?"

"Nope."

Knowing my pal as I did, I figured that Soup was about to be sentenced to a term of two weeks that would actual seem a whole lot closer to two years.

"We could climb up into the barn rafters and then jump down in the hay," I said. "Maybe you'd like to do that, Sexton. Would ya?"

"No," he said, "I wouldn't."

Right then, I noticed that Soup was poking a hand to fish something up from one of his trouser pockets. Out came his rusty old harmonica. Whacking it on his leg a few times, Soup spooked a few loose grains of grit from the holes.

"Here," said Soup, trying to hand the harmonica to his cousin, "I betcha go for music, Sexton. Everybody likes a tune or two."

"I don't," said Sexton Dilly.

Without another word, Soup blew a few sour notes on his harmonica, which he still hadn't quite mastered, then stuffed the instrument back inside his pocket.

"How was that?" he asked his cousin.

"Dreadful," said Sexton.

Well, I was thinking, maybe Soup's harmonica music wasn't too pleasant to ear at. But one thing for certain, there were worse noises around. One of the worst, I thought, was the sound of Sexton's voice. He didn't talk. He squawked. Sexton Dilly, I soon decided, was about as much fun as an all-night dentist.

From the corner of my eye, I could see that Soup Vinson was about to blow his patience. If there was one thing Soup didn't go for, it was being told that he was a rotten harmonica player, even if he was.

"What can *you* do?" Soup asked him.

Sexton smiled. "I can swear."

Two

Soup blinked.

As he did it, I felt a grin growing on my face. Mainly because *swearing* was about the last activity in the world that I'd ever expect Sexton Dilly to handle.

However, from what I then saw and heard, Soup was not easily impressed. "I wouldn't actual call swearing a genuine talent," he told Sexton.

"Soup's right," I added. "Anybody can cuss."

Sexton smiled again, shoving both hands into his velvet pockets as though he really knew that he was about to perform a feat of stardom.

"Not," he said to me, "the fancy way *I* swear."

"Honest?" asked Soup.

"Honest," said Sexton. "When I put my mind to it, I can sometimes link a batch of oaths together like a

11

string of pearls. I can swear for one entire minute without repeating one single word."

"Wow" I said, beginning to sniff what Sexton Dilly was cooking. "I'd bet that even Eddy Tacker couldn't swear for an entire minute."

At school, whenever Miss Kelly was out of earshot, which wasn't very doggone often, Eddy was our champion cusser. That is, among us boys. Overall, first prize had to go, hands down, to Janice Riker. Some of Janice's words were so filthy that they smelled worse than a wet dog.

On more than one occasion, I vividly recalled, Miss Kelly had marched Janice Riker over to our washstand. There she made Janice stick out her tongue, to receive a gloppy lick of Octagon bar soap. It was yellowy-brown and tasted, according to a direct report from Janice, a lot more dirty than clean.

"I suppose," said Soup, "you think you can swear fancier than I can."

"Much," said Sexton.

From the doubting expression on Soup's face, I could see that he was not yet fully convinced as to Sexton Dilly's gifted vocabulary. I wasn't convinced either. "Okay," I said, "let's hear ya."

"No," said Sexton. He shook his head.

"How come?" Soup asked him.

"Because."

Soup snorted. "That's no reason."

Sexton shot us another sly smirk, flashing teeth that

looked as if they had been brushed at least thirty times a day. But then he did something that I wasn't at all prepared to witness. Slowly he pulled a hand out of one pocket, holding it out, palm up, in Soup's direction.

"I charge a penny," said Sexton.

Soup's mouth popped open. So did mine. I couldn't believe what I was hearing or seeing.

Soup looked down at his cousin's extended palm, then up at his face. "You mean to tell me that you actual *charge* kids a penny to listen to you *cuss?*"

Sexton calmly closed his eyes, then nodded. "No penny," he softly said, "no swearing."

It was then that Soup looked at me. "Got a penny, Rob?"

"Hold it," said Sexton Dilly. "Let's get it straight, shall we? If I swear, it'll be a penny from each one of you. Two cents, or no show."

Sexton leaned on a fender of his father's car and waited. Not knowing quite what to say next, I just stood there, looking at Soup. My pal's face was a picture of freckled curiosity. Inside, I really wanted to hear Sexton cuss. So I fished out a dirty penny to drop into Sexton's spotless and waiting hand. Soup did the same.

"Okay," Soup told him. "Fire away."

As he pocketed our two pennies into his pants, Sexton slowly shook his head. "Not here. I could be overheard."

"Where?" I asked.

With a casual turn of his head, Sexton Dilly looked over at Soup's red barn. Then he pointed. "Maybe over in there."

The two of us, Soup and I, followed Sexton toward the barn. The three of us went inside. Sexton looked around, then he climbed up to stand on the closed lid of an oat bin.

"This will do," he said, smiling down at Soup and me. "Maybe," said Sexton, "the two of you would like to take seats. After all, I do put on quite an exhibition. Especially for amateurs."

"You better be doggone good," said Soup.

Sexton presented us with a slight bow. "Oh, you'll both get your penny's worth, Luther."

Luther? I couldn't believe what I'd heard. Nobody, not even *me*, called Soup by his irregular name. If there was one word in the entire English language that Soup hated, it was Luther. So I waited for Soup to blister Sexton's nose. Yet he didn't. Maybe he was too anxious to hear his cussing cousin.

"Well," said Soup, "crank up your swearing."

Sexton held up a hand. "First," he said quietly, "I'd favor a drink of water. You couldn't ask anyone to swear for an entire minute with a dry throat, could you?"

With a shrug, I trotted outside to the pump, worked it, and then toted a dipper of water for Sexton Dilly.

"Obliged," he said.

14

Raising the dipper to his lips, Sexton helped himself to a sip, a swallow, and finally did one thing more. Tossing back his head, he let out a long, gurgling gargle. Then he spat out the used water, shook the dipper dry, and flipped it to me.

I dropped it. The blue-speckled dipper hit the barn floor with a hollow clank. Bending over, I picked it up again.

"Now," said Soup, "let's hear ya swear."

"Yeah," I added. "We want our penny's worth."

Sexton, still standing up on the oat bin, appeared to be unhurried. "Please be seated, gentlemen," he said.

Soup and I sat on a crate. Up on the dusty bin, Sexton Dilly took half a step to the rear of his modest little stage. As Soup and I waited, he cleared his throat for our attention.

"Swear," said Soup.

Sexton nodded. "Indeed. But first, a word or two of introduction. Swearing, as you both shall soon hear, is not only a hobby. For me, it has become a profession. Fools swear for free. But wise men swear for profit."

I looked at Soup as he turned his head to look at me. There certainly was no disputing Sexton's latest claim. Soup and I had paid the price of admission. Two whole cents.

Sexton continued with an easy wave of his velveted arm. "To cuss is an art. Few people can do it with perfection. And, seeing as it's the only thing I'm really good at, I decided to do it well."

"Come on," Soup growled. "Give."

Sexton pretended not to notice Soup's heckling. Instead, his eyes stared upward, as though waiting for a cue of inspiration.

"I can swear," said Sexton, "like a cowboy. Or like a sailor at sea. Even like a sergeant in the army. But my masterpiece is my ability to swear like Donald Duck."

This I couldn't wait to hear. Donald Duck happened to be one of my very favorite cartoon personalities, whenever Soup and I could dig up a dime for the Saturday picture show. We liked Donald Duck in the Sunday funny papers too.

"Let's hear ya," I said.

Sexton smiled. "Here goes." Drawing in a deep breath, Sexton let loose. And I had to admit, from the very first *quack*, that Sexton Dilly's swearing was worth far more than a penny. It was worth a nickel, a dime, plus a quarter. Maybe even a whole dollar.

"KZTYPTD QMP XP TLDPRZ XWKL PDBCF FFT SHLTY DMPN RTFBG HZT KX JPMWXKGZ PDG. . . ."

Never, not even once in my entire life, had I ever heard anybody, kid or grown-up, swear for an entire minute and sound exactly like a very angry Donald Duck. In color! Some of the words I could almost recognize. Others were total strangers. Yet I had to admit that Sexton Dilly was the world's champion cusser.

"Wow," whispered Soup.

The two of us clapped our hands with reverent appreciation as Sexton smiled and took a bow. Then, for an encore, he delivered a few extra blasts of profanity. In regular English.

Soup stood up.

"Sexton," he said, walking a step or two over to where his cousin still stood atop the oat bin, "do you think you could actual *teach* somebody to swear like you do?"

Hopping lightly down from his stage, Sexton smiled modestly. "Of course," he told us. "Rather easily."

"Honest?" I asked.

"Absolutely."

"For free?" Soup asked his cousin.

"Not a chance," said Sexton.

Three

"Germany," said Miss Kelly.

Our teacher was standing at the side of our classroom, holding a blackboard eraser and using her long pointer to tap a wall map of Europe.

"Now then, the people who live in this country," Miss Kelly continued to say, "are called—"

"Germs," said Janice.

I saw Miss Kelly haul in a deep breath, and then, as though she were silently counting, let it out slowly. Janice Riker, we all knew, was not exactly the brightest kid in our one-room school. However, what Janice lacked in wits, Miss Kelly evened the score with patience.

Nobody ever laughed when Janice yelped out a stupid answer because Janice Riker possessed not only the smallest brain but also the biggest, hardest, and fastest fist. She was also quite chunky and built lower to the ground than a septic tank.

"I know they're germs," Janice went on to say, "because, last year, I took sick with German weasels."

"Measles," said Miss Kelly.

"Yeah," said Janice with a nod. "I had *them* too.

Dots all over my face. If I get 'em again, I'll bring 'em to school, for Show and Tell."

Outside, a car honked.

As she looked out the window, our teacher smiled and waved to our approaching visitor. But then the smile on her face seemed to melt into an expression of total amazement. I saw Miss Kelly drop her eraser.

In walked Miss Boland, our county nurse, but she didn't come alone. She was leading a little white goat.

"Howdy, you all," she boomed.

"*Blaaa,*" the goat bleated.

Compared to the tiny little goat, or to anything else, Miss Boland was a very large lady. She and Miss Kelly were close friends, like Soup and me. As usual, her nursing uniform made Miss Boland look whiter than a long winter and nearly the same size.

I grinned. Because whenever Miss Boland popped in at our schoolhouse, she usual brought a hot hunk of news.

"This," said Miss Boland, "is a goat."

Miss Kelly raised one eyebrow. "So I see."

"And," said Miss Boland, "you're probable all wondering why I've bothered to lug a goat to school."

Miss Kelly said, "Well, now that you mention it, the thought *did* cross my mind."

Our country nurse began to crack a smile. "It's all because of a week from this Saturday."

"Oh," said Miss Kelly. Her face, however, still seemed anxious to ask her friend a few more details.

Before answering, Miss Boland led the little white

goat by a rope around in one complete circle. Then she leaned down to scratch the goat's head.

"You see," said Miss Boland, "next week is Pet Week. As you know, every year we feature a particular animal. Last year, you'll remember, it was cats. And the cat show was a great success until *somebody* let loose all those mice."

Miss Kelly looked over at Soup and me without saying a word.

"Steady," whispered Soup. "She doesn't know for certain. She only *suspects.*"

"She knows," I whispered back. Of this, I was positive. Miss Kelly not only knew about our mice, she also knew we knew she knew.

"Now," said Miss Boland as she continued to parade her goat around Miss Kelly's desk, "are you ready to hear *my great idea?*"

"If I can take it," Miss Kelly said.

"This year," said Miss Boland, pointing a chubby finger into the air, "the animals we feature will be—"

"Weasels?" asked Janice.

"No," said Miss Boland. "Goats."

Miss Kelly said, "My, I never would have guessed."

"But," said Miss Boland, "you've only heard a portion of my entire plan. We're going to have a goat race a week from Saturday, right through town."

All of us kids cheered.

Gee, I was thinking, a goat race might really turn out to be a whole lot of fun. Meanwhile, our teacher was laughing. She turned to her friend.

"And," she asked, "is this goat the unfortunate little steed *you're* planning to ride?"

Miss Boland's face pretended to fade serious. *"Me? Ride him?* Don't be absurd. Besides, the goat race isn't for grown-ups. It's for *kids!"*

Again we cheered.

"We get to ride *goats?"* asked Soup.

Our nurse shook her head. "You don't *ride* a goat. You *drive* one. You'll build your own goat cart and select a goat to pull it in the race. Why, back when I was a youngster, goat races were right popular."

"Is that true, Miss Kelly?" I asked.

Our teacher nodded. "Indeed so, Robert. Needless to say, the goats that trotted the carts were quite a bit larger than this one. By the way, what's your pet's name?" she asked our nurse.

Miss Boland smiled. "Gordon. But he's really not mine. He belongs to Arno Fletcher. You know, the gent who owns the Billy-the-Kid Goat Farm. I've already talked Arno into lending us a few of his biggest, strongest, and fastest goats for the race a week from Saturday."

As Gordon started to nibble at the eraser that lay on the floor, Miss Kelly looked at all of us.

"Class," she said. "I think we owe our friend Miss Boland a big round of applause. Don't you?"

We all clapped, except for Gordon, who continued to gobble the eraser.

Then, because we were told that there weren't quite enough racing goats to go around, we all threw our names into a hat. Miss Kelly drew out the five winners; and then, as I held my breath, she announced the five lucky kids.

"Our winners," said Miss Kelly, "are . . . Ally Tidwell, Luther Vinson, Eddy Tacker, Janice Riker, and . . . Robert Peck."

Even though there were a few groans from all the kids whose names had not been selected, I could hardly breathe. "Wow," I said to Soup, "we *both* get to enter ourselves in the goat race."

Soup sort of smiled. "I'll beatcha," he told me. "I just know my goat is going to run faster than yours."

"Like heck," I told Soup.

"Wait and see," he said.

Up front, Miss Boland and Miss Kelly were trying to restore order, in spite of all the excitement about the upcoming goat race. Our nurse calmly held up her hand, requesting that we control our enthusiasm.

"After school," said Miss Boland, "I'll tote you five winners out to the goat farm where you'll be able to select your goats for the race."

We nodded.

Miss Kelly, for some strange reason, was again smiling. I didn't know exactly why.

"How," she asked Miss Boland, "do you intend to squeeze five children, and Gordon, not to mention yourself, into that little car of yours?"

"We'll do it," Miss Boland shot back. "Even if we have to chuck out the engine."

"*Blaaa,*" said Gordon.

Four

"All aboard," said Miss Boland.

Her car was a Hoover. According to some of our local car experts, it was the smallest car in town. The car almost looked smaller than Miss Boland. Most things did.

Inside, the car supplied barely enough room to accommodate its enormous owner. Yet the word *impossible* didn't belong in Miss Boland's vocabulary. When something in our town of Learning *couldn't* be done, it was usual our county nurse who insisted it *could* be. Then did it.

The Hoover was what Miss Boland called a *coop.* An apt name. It didn't have a backseat. And once our driver had finally squeezed behind the wheel, the Hoover no longer had much of a front seat either.

"I can't breathe," said Janice.

Soup and I were sitting on the laps of Eddy Tacker and Ally Tidwell, both of whom were seated on Janice Ricker, who had jumped in first.

"Hold it," said Miss Boland. "We forgot Gordon."

With a grunt, she climbed out of the car and then stuffed Gordon, kicking and bleating, through the passenger window to Soup and me. Then she squeezed herself back in, abused the engine, and we were off.

"Miss Boland," I heard Janice groan. "I gotta go to the bathroom."

"So does Gordon," said Soup.

"No, he doesn't," I said. "Not anymore." The eraser, I then presumed, had begun to give Gordon more than only a few symptoms of digestive distress.

How we finally got all the way to Mr. Arno Fletcher's goat farm, I'll never know. It wasn't too joyous a journey. Everyone, including Gordon, seemed determined to change places with somebody else.

To make our conditions of travel more complicated, and less than fragrant, whatever it was that Gordon had to do, he had already done.

I even thought that I'd heard Miss Boland utter a word, in a whisper, that Sexton Dilly might have used. Yet her word was relatively mild, by comparison, to some of the muffled ones that came from Janice, on the bottom of our pile.

"We're here," Miss Boland announced at last.

I needed air. It had been at least ten minutes since my last breath. But, considering the Hoover's internal atmospheric quality, due to Gordon's breath and other gastric contributions, inhaling was hardly a luxury.

"All of you—*out*," Miss Boland grunted. "And whatever's left over is *me*."

For obvious reasons of personal emergency, Janice Riker was determined to get out first. To her, the old rule of *first in, last out* held little appeal. Punching, kicking, and biting, Janice fought her way upward through Eddy, Ally, Soup, me, and Gordon.

"I won," Janice loudly proclaimed.

No one disagreed. Nobody dared. Not a kid in our school wanted to cross Janice even when she was in a *good* mood, which was never. If you crossed Janice, you'd get a cross in return. The Red Cross. Fighting with Janice, I had sorrowfully learned, was about as much fun as punching a fire hydrant.

Mr. Fletcher greeted us all with a friendly grin. The five of us selected our goats for the race. Janice, because ladies always go first, got first choice.

She picked a big goat named Geronimo.

Eddy chose Hector. Ally selected Winthrop. Soup's choice was a black and white goat whose name, according to Mr. Fletcher, was Orbit. My goat was black and white too. His name was Nesbit.

"My goat's the biggest one," said Janice.

Nobody argued.

Mr. Fletcher escorted us into his barn to show us what a goat cart looked like. His was bright yellow with red wheels. It looked small, light, and very fast.

"Remember," said Miss Boland, "part of the fun is building your own goat cart."

Soup sighed.

Work, I had observed, was not Luther Wesley Vinson's favorite pastime. Not that Soup was afraid of a dose of work. If *I* was doing it, he'd watch for hours.

Miss Boland, along with the three other kids, were all paying close attention to Mr. Fletcher as he described the details of goat cart construction. Soup, however, did not appear overly interested.

"Rob, look over there," he whispered.

I looked. In a dark corner of Mr. Fletcher's barn stood another goat cart. This one looked several sizes bigger than the yellow cart we'd first seen. Soup was now eyeing it with increasing enthusiasm.

"Maybe," he said. "Just possible maybe."

"No," I whispered to Soup. "Whatever it is you're thinking, don't think it."

"Think what?"

"We're *not*," I told Soup, "going to sneak back here to the goat farm, in the dark of night, and *borrow* that big cart." I paused. "Are we?"

There was, I could now sense by the expression on Soup's face, a plan hatching in his brain. While others sweated, Soup schemed. That was his style, I knew, so there was really no hope in ever trying to reform him.

I smelled trouble.

As I took a deep breath I could also smell traces of Gordon; but, for some reason, the *trouble* that I knew Soup would try to talk me into smelled worse.

"I'm gonna win the race," I overheard Janice Riker say. "Because I got Geronimo, and he's the biggest and strongest goat."

"Do ya think that's true?" I asked Soup.

Slowly, he shook his head. "Rob, old top, there's one thing ya gotta learn in life."

"What's that?"

"It ain't always the biggest goat that's bound to win a goat race."

"Who *does* win?" I asked Soup.

He smiled. "The biggest *brain.*"

"So," said Mr. Fletcher, "that's how you build yourselves a goat cart. Oh, it may sound like a lot of work but it's a barrel of fun. Once you get your teeth into it."

Janice, who had gotten *her teeth* into all of us at one time or another, then announced that she would build the *biggest* cart. As he listened, Soup shot me a wink. Then he turned to Janice Riker.

"I bet," he said to Janice, "that the bigger a goat cart is, the faster it races."

As he said it, I could tell by the tone of his voice that Soup was already plotting up a scheme.

We all left the barn to drift outside into the afternoon sunlight. All five of us wanted to visit our goats again. As I leaned on the pasture fence, I noticed something that I hadn't took note of earlier. I scratched my head.

"Say," I asked Soup, "which goat is mine, and which one is yours?"

Soup pointed. "That one there is Orbit."

"Maybe so," said Mr. Fletcher, "and maybe no."

"How come?" Soup asked him.

"Well," said Mr. Fletcher, resting a boot on the lower rail of the fence, "ya see, Orbit and Nesbit are twins. There's only one way to tell 'em apart."

I waited. So did Soup.

"Nesbit's nice, but Orbit's ornery mean."

Five

We waved good-bye.

Miss Boland, along with Eddy, Ally, and Janice, piled into her Hoover and went chugging away from Mr. Arno Fletcher's goat farm. Because the two of us lived nearby, Soup and I decided to walk home.

"Well," I told Soup, "maybe we best get ourselfs headed for home. So we don't miss chores."

"Not quite yet," said Soup.

"How come?"

Soup pointed. "See those ducks?"

I looked. Sure enough, there sat a flock of white ducks at the edge of a small pond in Mr. Fletcher's meadow.

"It might work," said Soup.

"What might?"

Soup looked around. Mr. Arno Fletcher, owner and proprietor of the Billy-the-Kid Goat Farm, was nowhere in view. A second later, Soup vaulted over the fence, into the goat pasture.

"Let's go, Rob."

"Okay," I said, climbing over the fence.

Soup walked toward where the white ducks were taking life quietly. They did, however, rise to their orange feet, the closer we walked. Some began to flutter away.

"Now," said Soup, "we'll find out."

"About what?"

"Oh," he told me, "you'll see. It's something I heard, one time, about ducks and goats."

As I followed along with Soup, he cautiously circled around the ducks so they wouldn't escape into the pond. I wondered what his plan was. Ducks? It didn't make a whole batch of sense to me. Nonetheless, I tagged along after my pal, knowing full well he had a reason for duck herding.

"All we do now," he said, "is sort of mosey the ducks over to where the goats are. Simple as pie."

"What for?"

Soup winked. "To learn something. If it pans out, maybe it'll save us a whole batch of work."

The closer we trotted toward the ducks, the faster they waddled, exactly as Soup had planned, toward the goats.

"Now!" said Soup.

I couldn't believe what I then saw and heard. Soup ran toward the ducks flapping his arms, and doing one more thing. He *quacked*. So did the ducks as they scattered toward the goats.

I was surprised. But, I had to admit, Mr. Fletcher's goats were suddenly acting a lot more surprised than I was. Some jumped up into the air and bleated. Others bolted. But then *all* the goats took off faster than if they'd been chased by Janice Riker.

"See?" asked Soup, a bit out of breath from all his running and quacking.

"So what?" I asked him. "If Mr. Fletcher catches us spooking his ducks, not to mention his goats, I don't guess he'll give us any more advice on how to construct our goat carts."

Soup grinned.

As the two of us continued across the meadow toward home, I could see the smile on Soup's face starting to widen.

"Yup," he said as the two of us climbed another fence, exiting from Mr. Fletcher's pasture, "it just might figure in."

I couldn't stand it any longer. All I knew was that Luther Wesley Vinson, my troublemaking pal, had come up with a tricky plan that involved both ducks and goats. Worse yet, his plan would no doubt involve me. Up, as usual, to my neck.

"What might work, Soup?"

Soup laughed. "I can hardly wait."

"For what?" As I asked the question, I was already aware that the light bulb of trickery was already flickering inside Soup's brain.

"The goat race," said Soup as we were cutting through a small patch of maple trees, heading for home. Reaching up for a low branch, Soup swung himself up, tucked his body into a skin-the-cat, and dropped.

I tried to do it too. But I didn't quite pull it off with an agility equal to Soup's.

"Okay," I told Soup, "out with it. You're planning to tote along a few ducks, hidden in your goat cart, aren't ya?"

"Nope, not me."

"I don't believe it, Soup. You're up to something, and I want to know what it is. Right sudden."

Soup grinned. "Rob, old top, what I'm fixing to do," he said, "doesn't have anything whatsoever to do with Mr. Fletcher's ducks."

"Honest?"

Soup nodded. "Cross my heart. All I wanted was to learn if a duck could actual spook a goat."

"That's all?"

"Well," said Soup, "maybe a bit more."

Jumping over Harley's Crick, the two of us ran up the bank, took the shortcut through Mrs. Dooley's grape vines, and were now coming to my house. Soup still hadn't confided in me a whole bunch. Whatever he knew, he was harboring to himself.

In a way, I felt a bit relieved.

For several years, a good number of Soup Vinson's plans had led to nothing but disaster for Robert Peck. At least this time, I thought, I had managed to dodge the bullet. Yet I knew it couldn't last. Sooner or later, Soup would unfold his plan.

I stopped.

"Doggone it, Soup. You know darn well I'm itching to find out about your scheme. If I don't learn it soon, I'll lie awake all night and fret."

"No you won't."

In my mind, I could still see Soup, running toward that flock of white ducks, flapping his arms and quacking. Yet it was still a total mystery, to me, how a duck could possible fit into a plan for winning a goat race. It didn't add up.

"Ducks?" I asked Soup again.

He punched me, not hard. "No," he said with a slightly evil smile. "Not ducks. Just *one duck.*"

"One?"

"Rob, old timer, just one duck is all we'll use."

One duck, I was thinking. Maybe Soup's idea was to hitch up a duck to his goat cart, alongside of Orbit, his goat. No, I concluded, that didn't make any reason. But then, very little of Soup's schemes ever made any sense at all. Until it was too late for me to count myself out.

"Okay," I asked, "which duck is it?"

Soup hopped over a fallen log.

"Well," he said, turning around to face me, "if you really gotta know, I'll give ya a clue."

"Shoot."

"The duck I plan to use doesn't have any white feathers on it."

I stood looking at Soup. He seemed unconcerned. All he did was climb up and walk back and forth on the fallen log, holding his arms out for balance.

"No white feathers?" I asked.

Soup winked. "Not a one."

"What color feathers *does* it have?"

"No feathers at all."

I scratched my head again. A duck without any feathers. Was good old Soup planning to pluck a duck? Whatever he was planning, the two of us would, as always, end up as a couple of dead ducks.

Soup sat, to straddle the log. "Give up?"

I shrugged. "There's no way we can use a dead duck to win a goat race. Is there?"

36

"Hold it, Rob. I never said the duck's dead."

"It's alive?"

Soup laughed. "Oh, he's alive all right. And, old sport, you even know his name."

"Okay, wise guy. What's the duck's name?"

Soup grinned. "Sexton."

Six

Bloop!

I heard a funny noise.

It wasn't really music. Instead it sort of sounded as though an elephant, with a bad cold and a sore throat, was burping.

Bloop!

As we were all seated in school, behind our desks, we knew better than to jump up and race over to the open window to look outside. Miss Kelly would *not* condone such a stampede. She, however, *did* look out the window. Right before she dropped our arithmetic papers.

"I don't believe it," she said.

Before any of us had a chance to ask Miss Kelly what she'd witnessed, in bounced Miss Boland. But, instead of her usual white nurse's cap, on her head was a very strange hat. She was carrying the largest musical instrument I'd ever seen, other than a piano. It was silver, with about a mile of twisting pipes, three fingering valves, plus a giant golden bell. Drawing in a deep breath, Miss Boland blew into her instrument one more time.

Bloop!

"What on earth?" Miss Kelly finally asked.

"It's my old *tuba*," said Miss Boland.

"So I see. But you haven't played the tuba for years. And, if I may ask, what in the name of insanity is that *thing* on your head?"

"It's a helmet," Miss Boland said. "The kind explorers wear whenever they go exploring in jungles. I believe it's called a *pith* helmet."

"It looks like *pith* to me," whispered Soup, a remark that our teacher had, luckily, not heard.

Before she could faint, Miss Kelly sat herself down in the chair behind her big brown desk. "And," she then asked Miss Boland, "I presume we're all to inquire *why* you're wearing a pith helmet and blooping your old tuba?"

Miss Boland beamed. "He's *coming!*"

"Good," agreed Miss Kelly. "He's coming from the asylum to take you away for a very long rest?"

"You'll never guess," said Miss Boland, presenting us all with one more *bloop* on the tuba, "who's coming to town."

"No, I never shall."

Miss Boland smiled. "Frank Sumatra!"

"Who is *he*?"

Our nurse almost broke into a dance. "Well, in case you don't know, Dr. Frank Sumatra just happens to be the world's most famous South Seas explorer. As a boy, years ago, he played the tuba. He's also a leading authority on *goats*. And he's coming to town. Right here to Learning."

"You're sure?" asked Miss Kelly.

Bloop! came the answer. "He also," Miss Boland informed us, "happens to be—*very handsome.*"

With an understanding toss of her head, Miss Kelly laughed at the ceiling. "Ah," she commented at last, "the skies are beginning to clear."

Norma Jean Bissell raised her hand with the grace of a fairy princess. I sighed. Soup heard me and pretended he was about to be sick. I didn't care, because Norma Jean was a girl who could easily make me either ache or tingle all over.

"Miss Boland," she said in a voice more melodic than a cello, "why is Dr. Sumatra coming to town?"

"'To preside," said Miss Boland, "on Goat Day, which is, as all of you already know, a week from this coming Saturday. The whole thing was *my* idea."

"So I assume," said Miss Kelly.

Miss Boland nodded. "Dr. Sumatra's a friend of Arno's, who helped me to arrange it all."

"I'm surprised," said Miss Kelly, "that you're not planning to greet our distinguished South Seas explorer wearing a grass skirt."

I could see, by the enthusiastic gleam in Miss Boland's eyes, that her eagerness to meet Dr. Frank Sumatra would not be dampened.

"That's only part of the surprise," she said. "The best part is *this.*"

"I can't wait," said Miss Kelly in a voice that almost pictured Miss Boland in a grass skirt, one that would need at least half of the grass in Vermont.

"Dr. Sumatra's *favorite song,*" Miss Boland went on to say, "also happens to be *my* very favorite."

Miss Kelly asked, "Which is?"

" 'A Tropical Moon and You.' "

As she announced the song's title, I again stole a glance at Norma Jean Bissell. In my imagination, I was a South Seas explorer; Norma Jean was a coffee-skinned island maiden, adorning my neck with a garland of flowers, her eyes shyly gazing up at me, twin pools of limpid promise.

Bloop!

The explosion of Miss Boland's tuba jolted me back to Vermont and school.

"Kids," said Miss Boland. "I'm going to ask all of you to do me, or rather do our town, one heck of a big favor."

We all agreed we'd do it. After all, Miss Boland was a regular pal of ours as well as Miss Kelly's.

"All you'll have to do," said Miss Boland, reaching into the giant golden bell of her tuba to unfold a sheet of music, "is to learn to sing this haunting melody. Here it is! 'A Tropical Moon and You.'"

Miss Boland unrolled her music and *blooped* out the tune. It sounded about as tropically romantic as a sick moose who had fallen in love with a factory whistle. It really wasn't haunting. It was hurting.

I saw Miss Kelly grit her teeth.

Nonetheless, no one interrupted until our nurse and her ancient tuba had finally allowed "A Tropical Moon and You" to come wheezing to its last merciful *bloop*.

We all clapped, because it was over.

As Miss Boland gave us a modest bow of her head, Miss Kelly said, "I'm sure the children will be able to sing it every bit as well as you played it. May we hope, even better."

"I know it's a lot to ask," panted Miss Boland, her face still beet red from her tuba blowing, "so I'll not request that the five of you who are to construct goat carts learn the song."

"Thank gosh," I heard Soup whisper.

Again I saw Norma Jean Bissell raise her hand to speak. I listened with rapt adoration.

"Will we have to sing the song all alone?" she asked Miss Boland.

"No, my dear. All the while you're singing, I'll be

right there to accompany all of you. On the tuba."

Miss Kelly winced.

"I'm sure," our teacher hurriedly said, "we'll be able to learn to sing 'A Tropical Moon and You' by next weekend. However, with all *you* have to do," she said to our nurse, "it might be asking too much to insist that you also play the tuba."

Miss Boland looked slightly wounded. "But," she insisted, "as I told you earlier, the tuba was Dr. Frank Sumatra's boyhood instrument. Just hearing me play it will inspire Dr. Sumatra to *escape* back to the golden days of childhood. Don't you agree?"

"Yes," said Miss Kelly, "escape."

Miss Boland made a slight frown. "Well, so maybe I'm a bit rusty. But my old lip is still in shape. Even though the rest of me isn't."

Turning to us, Miss Kelly said, "Class, just think. We're actually having a famous South Seas explorer coming to Learning for Goat Day. Won't that be exciting?"

"Yes," sighed Miss Boland.

"I meant," said Miss Kelly, "for the youngsters."

"Oh, I just hope you'll all be able to learn—*our song*—in time for Frank's—I meant to say Dr. Sumatra's arrival."

"We will," said Norma Jean Bissell.

Closing my eyes, I could envision Norma Jean, wearing a grass skirt and perhaps strumming a ukulele, singing "A Tropical Moon and You" to me alone.

44

Her face was bathed in moonlight, and the night was perfumed by South Sea island flowers.

"Norma Jean," I gently whispered to my vision.

"I'm throwing up," said Soup.

Seven

"Do I have to?" Soup asked.

"Yes," his mother told him, "you have to."

It was Saturday morning. We were at Soup's house; Sexton Dilly, his cussing cousin, was upstairs. Soup and I stood in his kitchen, demolishing a few sloppy peanut butter and jelly sandwiches and neatly wiping our hands on each other.

"Luther, I think it would be proper," said Mr. Vinson, "if you and Robert took Sexton on a hike out to Mr. Fletcher's place to show him the racing goats."

Soup sighed. "Okay, we'll let Sexton tag along. But he isn't a whole bunch of *fun*. Maybe I'll leave him there."

Mrs. Vinson's eyes narrowed. "If you *dare* to come

back without him, what your *bottom* will get, out in the woodshed, won't be *any fun at all.*"

"Yes'm," said Soup.

After we'd waited for about twenty years, Sexton finally came downstairs. His hair was so plastered that it appeared as though he used wallpaper paste. He was so washed that he looked *new*, all over.

Soup's mother smiled at him. "You'd like to go along with the boys to see the goats, wouldn't you, Sexton?"

"No," said Sexton.

"He doesn't want to go," said Soup.

"Aw, come on along, Sexton," I said, just to torture Soup. "It really isn't very far. You won't get dirty."

"You have peanut butter on your mouth," Sexton told me. He winced as I wiped it off with my sleeve. "Luther has jelly on his shirt."

Mrs. Vinson sighed. "Would *you* like a nice peanut butter and jelly sandwich, Sexton?"

"Not really," the kid replied. "It'll stick to the roof of my mouth."

"The peanut butter?"

"No," Sexton answered her. "The jelly."

"Well, let's be away," Soup groaned.

The three of us started hiking in the direction of Mr. Arno Fletcher's Billy-the-Kid Goat Farm. Sexton didn't even *try* to keep up. Instead, he strolled about forty feet behind Soup and me, preferring, it was obvious, his own company to ours.

As we trudged along, I asked Soup a question in a low voice. "What do you guess Sexton's going to be when he grows up?"

"A bigger pain," said Soup. "Or a rainy day."

We arrived at the outskirts of the goat farm.

"Let's jump over the fence," Soup suggested, "and maybe we can locate our goats." He looked back over his shoulder. "Coming along, Sexton?"

"I suppose so," Sexton moaned. "Although, I must confess, goats do not interest me a whole lot."

"Don't worry," Soup told him. "You probable won't interest *them* a lot either."

About a minute after the three of us had entered the pasture, we spotted a few goats. They were placidly grazing underneath some low-hanging willows and elm trees. Two of the goats were black and white.

Soup pointed. "Look, there's Orbit."

"Are ya positive?" I asked. "He looks a bit more like *my* goat, Nesbit, to me."

Soup scratched his head. "Maybe so." He walked over to one of the black and white goats. I went too.

"You're right, Rob, old top. This is your goat, Nesbit. Pet him and make friends."

As I stretched out an amiable hand to stroke Nesbit, he bit my finger. Then butted and finally kicked at me. Three times.

"He's Orbit," said Soup with a sly smile.

"Okay," I said to Soup. "It's *your* turn. He's *your* goat, so go get friendly with ornery Orbit youself."

As I said it, I carefully walked over and began to pet Nesbit. He gave my face a friendly wet lick with his rough tongue. In fact, Nesbit acted so nice that he even allowed me to put my arms around his neck to hug him.

"See?" I said to Soup.

Soup was busy trying to pet Orbit, a goat with his ears back and his little horns lowered into butting position. Whirling, he kicked at Soup several times.

I smiled. "Orbit's ornery," I told Soup, "but, as you can plain see, old Nesbit here is sweeter than candy."

"Yeah," said Soup. "So I see."

I turned to look at Sexton. "Hey, ya wanna pet my goat?" I asked him. "Nesbit's nice."

"No," said Sexton. "He looks dirty."

"Maybe he is," I said, giving Nesbit another hug. "But at least he doesn't swear."

As I petted Nesbit, I looked over to check on what Soup was doing. Again he tried to be pals with Orbit. No dice. Obit, I could see, was one ornery goat. How my pal would ever harness and drive *him* could pose a major problem for Soup.

But right then I saw ornery Orbit suddenly do something that amazed the living heck out of me. He strolled slowly over to stand beside his twin brother, Nesbit. Orbit's ears came forward, and he darn near smiled. He even gave Nesbit a friendly nuzzle.

"I'll be a redtail rat," said Soup. "If old Orbit's near Nesbit, he don't look or act quite so meanish."

"Well," I said to Soup, "I reckon Orbit's *your* problem."

Soup grinned. "Rob, old sport, you seem to be a lot sharper at goat handling than I am. How would ya like to swap goats? I'll take Nesbit, and *you* can have Orbit. Okay?"

I shook my head. "No dice. Nesbit's *my* goat."

"Maybe," said Soup, as he sat down to lean his back against a pasture elm, "we might be able to work out a deal."

Hearing that, I smelled trouble again. Soup was up to something, which made me realize that I'd really have to be on guard. I wasn't going to swap. Yet maybe Soup was right. Perhaps I *was* better at handling goats. To prove it to myself, I reached over and patted Orbit and Nesbit, both at once.

"Look," I said. "As long as they stand side by side, you can't tell 'em apart. They're both good-tempered."

Sexton yawned.

"I got a nifty idea," said Soup.

"Like what?" I asked him as I calmly continued to pet both goats.

"It's a surprise," said Soup, "for later."

Soup and I stayed with the goats for about ten minutes. Sexton only watched and remained cleaner than a Sunday morn. Soup, meanwhile, got up from leaning against the elm tree to join Orbit, Nesbit, and me. He even petted Orbit who, this time, accepted Soup's friendship.

I saw Mr. Fletcher walking our way.

"Good morning, boys."

"Oh, hiya Mr. Fletcher," said Soup. "We stopped over to make friends with our goats. Because of the race a week from today."

Mr. Fletcher smiled. "Good idea."

"We just found something out," I told Mr. Fletcher. "Orbit, when he's standing next to his twin brother, acts as nice as Nesbit."

The goat man nodded. "He sure does."

"How come?" Soup asked him.

Mr. Fletcher then explained why. "Years ago," he told us, "those twin goats used to perform in a circus. After that, I bought 'em."

"Honest?" Soup asked.

"Right. Orbit and Nesbit used to be a goat team, and they'd pull a cart, carrying clowns, around in the circus ring. Until the circus broke up. Right after the big fire."

"Which fire?" I asked Mr. Fletcher.

"The circus burned. It happened right over in Cloonsburg, nearby. Mrs. Fletcher and I were there and saw it all. A terrible fire. Don't know how it started. Maybe some careless soul flicked a match into the elephant hay. Everybody escaped unharmed. But it sure destroyed the Big Top tent."

"Tell us about it," said Soup. "Please."

Mr. Fletcher took off his hat. "I'll never forget that evening if I survive to a hundred. It all happened so quicksome. The clowns and goats had just started their fun in the center ring. And the circus band, all dressed up in their spanky red uniforms, struck up a tune. Then the fire broke out."

"Wow!" I said.

"You never saw a pair of goats run as fast as Orbit and Nesbit did. No sir. These two goats took off, cart and all. Ran so rapid that they were the first ones out of the tent, to safety. Nope, I'll never forget that night. I will always remember the tune that the circus band had started to play."

"Which tune was it?" Soup asked Mr. Fletcher.

"It was 'A Tropical Moon and You.' "

Eight

Monday came.

Even though I was in school, at my desk, I felt real joyous. Only six more days until Goat Day and the big important race. I wondered if Saturday would ever arrive.

Nesbit and I were going to win that race, for certain sure, or my name wasn't Rob Peck.

Miss Kelly cleared her throat. "I have some very good news. Early this morning," she said, "Miss Boland came to school and deposited some material out back of our building."

"What kind of material?" Soup asked her.

Our teacher smiled. "I believe we could all go outside, right after geography, and see for ourselves."

Due to the suspense, geography only lasted for twenty-eight years.

Then, true to her word, Miss Kelly led us all out of the classroom to behind the school. Sure enough, all of it was there. Wheels! Lumber scraps! Wire! Plus about ten miles of clothesline for weaving our goat harnesses.

"I think it would be proper," Miss Kelly told us, "to allow the children who are *not* racing goats to help those who are, in building the goat carts. Don't you?"

"Yes," we all agreed, as every kid in the class surged forward to grab the best stuff.

"Take turns," she warned us, "and be sure to divide the material into five equal shares. Will you please?"

We all vowed we would.

But then, as soon as Miss Kelly had excused herself, to return inside to correct our geography papers, we all dived into the pile. The outcome was no surprise.

"I got the most!" said Janice Riker.

She was right. Janice had succeeded in cornering several wheels, half the lumber, and far more than her share of the rope. What she didn't grab, Eddy Tacker did. And it sure didn't leave a whole lot for Ally, Soup, and me. Not a one, among the three of us, was about to stand up to face Janice or Eddy, to demand our rights. Especially not against Janice Riker.

I sighed.

Janice was sometimes stupid and sometimes very tough. Yet, she was always Janice. I, for one, wasn't about to accuse her of hogging most of the supplies. But inside, my juices really sizzled. I wasn't merely angry. I was mad.

56

That was when I said—*the word!*

It was a *word* I'd never used before. Not until I had heard Soup's cousin, Sexton Dilly, cut loose with all of his gussy cussing. To be honest about it, I didn't rightly know exactly what *the word* meant.

But if ever a time was fitting to use it, the time was right now, with little or no stuff to build a goat cart.

"Robert Peck!"

I didn't have to turn around to know who had spoken my name. Miss Kelly heard me say—*the word.*

"Young sir," she then informed me, "you will remain after school, at which time we shall discuss manners. And vocabulary. Do you understand?"

"Yes'm."

It was almost an endless day.

With each echoing tick of the schoolroom's big wall clock, the hour of my doom, not to mention swift punishment, crept closer. *Tick. Tick. Tick. Tick.* The clock seemed to be almost repeating my *word.* Or rather, Sexton Dilly's word. I couldn't lay true claim to its creation.

School was finally over.

All the kids, except me, lined up to shake Miss Kelly's hand and to wish her a good night. Alone, I sat stuck to my bench as though my trousers were made of hot glue. To make matters worse, I itched, practically from head to toe. But mostly in the middle.

"The main problem with being a *kid*," Soup had once proclaimed to me, "is that you never get to select your own underwear."

I sat silently and scratched.

Soup was last in line and shot me a wink, as if to signal that he'd wait outside so that the two of us could walk uproad together. My eye tried to wink back. And flunked.

Miss Kelly closed the door.

So, there we were, Miss Kelly and me; two souls adrift in an almost silent schoolroom, except for the ticks of the school clock. I waited, knowing that she would be the first of us to determine the subject of our conversation.

She calmly sat down behind her giant desk, crooking a finger, demanding that I rise from mine and stand before the brown bench of judgment. The ruler on her desk looked bigger and bigger.

I came.

Miss Kelly stared. "Why do you scratch so much?"

"Because I'm the only one who knows where it itches."

As Miss Kelly looked very stern, I stopped scratching. But I sure didn't stop itching.

"Robert, today I heard you employ—a *word*—out back, behind the school."

I nodded.

"Are you sorry you used it?"

"Yes'm. And even sorrier you heard it."

Miss Kelly's face tightened. "I'm sure."

Inside, I was still itching. Not only my underwear. I was also itching to confess to Miss Kelly that I'd learned *the word* only recently, from Soup's cussing cousin, Sexton Dilly, when he swore like a duck. So she'd realize that it wasn't entirely my fault. But I didn't. Because I knew it wouldn't be fair to hang the blame around somebody else's neck.

As she sat very erect on her chair, Miss Kelly stared at me and asked, "Tell me, Robert, do you ever save things at home?"

"Yes'm."

"What do you save?"

"Bottle caps."

Miss Kelly almost smiled. "I see. Well, I try to save a great many things myself."

"What kinds of things?"

She sighed. "Mostly," she said, "I save memories. Faces, characters, and even a few ingenious pranks that represent all the boys and girls who have attended school here. Most of them are now grown up."

"I see."

"Good. Because I keep a tiny scrap from every child, to recall, and to cherish. I want very much to remember you, Robert. And to save something from you worth treasuring forever."

I swallowed. It wasn't too easy.

Miss Kelly leaned forward, touching both elbows to the surface of her desk, then lightly resting her chin on her interlaced fingers.

"Memories," she said, "are sweeter and so far more precious than a scrapbook. Or a photo album. What I choose to remember of you, Robert, will be the poem you wrote last year. I pasted a gold star on your paper."

"The one about the kittens?"

She nodded. "Yes. It was a very tender poem, and I'm still very proud of the *good* words you used. They were all—gold stars."

"Thank you."

"However, I shall ask you, young man, if you wish for me to remember the word you said today. Or would you prefer I remember the poem about the kittens that were born in your barn?"

"The kittens," I almost whispered. "Please."

"Very well. I shall ask something of you. Fill your memory, Robert, with kittens. So that someday your memory album will be golden, as shining to you as mine is for me. As shiny as a bottle cap."

"Yes'm." I said it like a prayer, because my heart really meant it so much.

"Never again?"

"No, Miss Kelly. Never, I promise."

"Good lad. In that case, I'll promise you that I shall remember your kittens."

I looked down at her ruler. For a moment, I really wanted Miss Kelly to crack me a smarter, because I'd hurt her by saying what I shouldn't have said.

She stood up. "All right, over to the washstand." I marched, following her all the way. "And now, close your eyes and stick out your tongue."

I wanted to tell her that the ruler would've been my choice, not the soap, but I couldn't quite muster up the courage. So, eyes closed, I stuck out my tongue, bracing for Octagon. But the yellowy-brown taste of that awful soap never came. Instead, I felt a light kiss on my cheek, as if an angel had planted it there.

Yet, when I finally opened my eyes, Miss Kelly was standing very straight and very tall. More like a church spire than a teacher.

"I'm sorry," I said. "Not so much because I said the word, but because it hurt your feelings to hear it."

Miss Kelly bit her lower lip. Only for an instant. Then she stood even straighter and told me to run along home. But before I raced out of the room, I did something that surprised both Miss Kelly and me. I just gave her a quick hug, harder than a bear.

Outside, Soup was waiting. He looked at me as if he was about to ask if I'd gotten the ruler. Yet, for some reason, he didn't fire a question. He kept quiet, for once. Maybe because he noticed that I was hurting. Then he punched me, but he didn't do it very hard. It was only a punch from a pal.

We didn't talk too much on the way home that afternoon. I wasn't in the mood for chatter. All I wanted was to remember Miss Kelly; not just for today, for always. Remembering her would be something worth saving.

Like a gold star.

Nine

It was Tuesday.

Miss Kelly dismissed us all from school an hour early so we could work on our goat carts.

Soup and I, on our way home, just happened to take a slightly different route. As we were sneaking by Janice Riker's house, a threatening pit of potential danger we habitually avoided, Soup pointed.

"Rob, looky yonder."

I looked.

Behind her house stood Janice's goat cart, complete with carriage, six wheels, a seat, two shafts (for both flanks of Geronimo, her goat) plus a harness.

"That's quite a machine," Soup admitted.

"Golly," I said, "it sure is. And we haven't even begun to start ours yet."

Janice's goat cart appeared not only to be large, it seemed to be built as sturdy as Janice Riker herself. It looked speedy. And it even had a name. *CHARGER* was boldly lettered on the side.

I sighed.

"With a nifty cart like that," I said, "I don't guess you or I got a chance of winning the goat race."

"Wrong," said Soup.

As he said it his face began to bloom into his usual we-can't-lose smile. I recognized the expression. It usual meant that Soup's brain was slowly giving birth to a plan, one that would eventually nudge the two of us toward either triumph or distaster. Or maybe ducks and goats.

Soup grinned. "Two against one," he said.

"I don't get it, Soup."

"Don't worry," he told me.

There it was! Soup's red flag of warning. Whenever he told me not to worry, that became my signal to substitute *dread* for both eating and sleeping.

We came to a fork in the road. Home lay in one direction, the right fork. Soup, however, calmly headed to the left. Turning, he flicked me a head-fake.

"*This* way, Rob."

"What for?"

"It's all a part of my grand idea."

With a useless shrug of my shoulders, both of which now slumped and sagged with surrender, I tagged along after Soup. He had quickened his pace and was stepping along with a determined resolution that only a genius, or a complete idiot, could strut.

"Where are we headed, Soup?"

"You'll see."

"But I want to know right *now*."

Without answering, Soup slowly lifted his eyes toward the sky, with a look of serene confidence and fervent belief. "Rob," he said, "in times of trial and trouble, we always have one place to turn to."

"Heaven?" I asked.

"No." Soup shot me a grin. "The Dump."

I should have known. In the past, The Dump was a place where the two of us had never failed to compose trouble. There was something about The Dump that guided our faithful little footsteps to its rusty gates.

"Well," said Soup at last, "here we are."

"Why?" I asked him.

Soup stared at me with a look of casual concern. "To build us a goat cart."

"You said *cart*, not carts."

Soup patted me on the back. "Congratulations, old bean," he said. "Building *one* cart will prove to be only *half the work* of constructing *two*."

Soup looked around.

"But," I said, "we've got *two* goats. You've got Orbit, and I got Nesbit."

Soup walked over to the pile of junk and began to tug on a silver handle. "Rob," he grunted, "there's no rule against what we're aiming to do."

"And what's that?"

"Come and help, so I can explain the details to you, so you'll understand."

I helped. As I tugged and strained on the silver handle, Soup, I noticed, eased his efforts to serve in mostly a supervisory capacity.

"Keep pulling," Soup told me.

I stopped. "What are *you* doing? Nothing?"

"Wrong," said Soup. "I'm thinking."

While he thought, I worked. It took me at least ten minutes to relocate various hunks of junk on top of the pile so that whatever was buried beneath could be freed. Yanking again on the silver handle, and coating my entire self with grit, dust, and odor, my straining finally paid off. I pulled *it* out. But couldn't believe what I saw.

It was a baby carriage. A big one. Soup removed the basket and discarded it, keeping only the frame, wheels, and handle.

"I *quit*," I told Soup. "That thing sure isn't going to be *my* goat cart."

"No," said Soup. "It isn't."

"*Yours*" I asked him.

"Nope. It's going to be *ours*," he said.

"Two of us, on *that old thing?*"

"Don't panic. That's only the frame. The base. All we need to locate now is the upper part we ride in."

I was still dirty and panting. Yet not too exhausted

or confused to ask Soup another question. "Why are we using a baby carriage?"

"Because," said Soup, "it's got four wheels. And one more important reason."

"Yeah? What's that?"

Soup gave the old vehicle a gentle pat with his hand. "A baby carriage will guarantee us a gentle ride. It's also got springs."

"Okay, but what'll we use for the rest of the cart?"

Soup glanced around The Dump. Watching, I wondered what he was searching for. Finding boards, he wired several on top of the base, for a platform. Then he climbed up the highest mountain of discarded junk.

"*Yahoo!*" he yelled. "Here it is!"

"What is it?"

With a wave of his arm, Luther Wesley Vinson was beckoning for me to climb up to where he stood.

"Come see. You won't believe it. And the name's already on it, which'll save us a whole lick of work."

At this point, I was thinking as I climbed up through the stink and the rubbish, I'd almost believe anything. Especially what an idiot I was to go along with one more of Soup's endless schemes of insanity.

"Hurry," said Soup.

Puffing, I made it to the top of the heap of trash. Soup rewarded my efforts with a sly grin.

"There she is," said Soup.

He pointed. I looked, blinked, and then resisted the

urge to slug him. Where he pointed lay a sign, the letters of which spelled out two words:

DIRTY LAUNDRY

"I don't believe you," I said. "You brought me all the way up here, on top of all this garbage, to peek at *that?*"

"Easy," said Soup. "That's only the *name* of our goat cart. What's important is what the sign is *on.*"

Squinting through the grit in both of my eyes, I saw. It was even worse. What I now looked at was the biggest and rattiest old hospital laundry basket I'd ever seen. The basket was much bigger than the baby carriage.

"That," said Soup, "is what we ride *in.*"

How we finally did it, I will never know. Our efforts were a combination of Soup's instructions and my sweat. But we did it. We sat the *DIRTY LAUNDRY* basket, which was gray canvas around a metal frame, onto the lower half of the baby carriage. Using an entire roll of black car-tape, which Soup had in his pocket, we secured everything in place. One wheel, however, wobbled a bit loose. We tightened the whole cart with strong wire, using some unbent old coat hangers.

"We need a longer handle," said Soup.

"What for?"

"For a shaft."

"Hold on," I told him. "A goat cart's got *two* shafts, to go on each side of the goat."

Soup sighed. "You're not thinking," he said. "This isn't going to be a *regular* goat cart. So all we need, old top, is just *one* shaft. In front, right straight up the middle."

I stared at my pal. Words wouldn't come. After all, what can anybody say to a lunatic?

"Ya see," said Soup, "one shaft is all part of my plan. There's something faster than just *one* goat."

"Oh? And what's that?"

"*Two* goats."

I tried not to digest what I was hearing. Soup had flipped. His brain had finally run out of gas, and it was now chugging merrily along on *Empty*. He removed the silver handle from the cart's base, tossing it away.

"Okay," said Soup. "Let's not waste time. We've got two more things to do. I'll poke around in the trash, locate some rope, and plan the harness."

I sort of groaned. "What'll I get?" I asked him.

Soup smiled. "You get the shaft."

Ten

Wednesday sped by.

Soup and I had returned, after school, to The Dump, where we added a few more final touches to *DIRTY LAUNDRY*, our racing cart.

But, as a result, I was late getting home for chores. Mama, Papa, and Aunt Carrie were not at all pleased. So, after supper was over, I was banished directly upstairs to tackle my homework.

"Bedtime," my mother later announced from the bottom of the stairs. "And I mean—*right now.*"

On my knees, I said my prayers, remembering to bless Papa, Mama, Aunt Carrie, Norma Jean Bissell, Miss Kelly, Mr. Arno Fletcher, along with Orbit and Nesbit. And then I added Dr. Frank Sumatra, Miss Boland, and Gordon.

Soup and God, I decided, were on their own.

Once my bedroom light was out, it didn't take me very long to say uncle to sleep. Even a shorter time to launch myself into a very pleasing dream about a certain somebody of whom I dreamed every night.

Norma Jean Bissell.

In my dream, there stood the two of us, high on a windy hilltop. Oddly, our pinnacle seemed to be the mountain of trash over at The Dump. Yet, somewhere, an orchestra was softly playing a love song. And, better yet, I was singing the lyrics to her in a mature baritone.

Leaning close, I inhaled the subtle fragrances of her hair.

"Norma Jean," I whispered to her, "you smell cleaner than a Sunday shirt."

"Rob," she whispered back, looking up into my eyes, "you smell like—*DIRTY LAUNDRY.*"

Undaunted, I looked over at the orchestra. All of the musicians seemed to be Miss Boland. And all of them were playing the tuba.

Bloop!

But then I heard another noise, one that was trying to awaken me and spoil my dream.

"Rob . . . Rob . . . Rob. . . ."

Opening my sleepy eyes, there I was, alone in my bedroom with no tubas, no dump, and no Norma Jean Bissell. But I kept on hearing my name. Worse yet, I knew who was whispering it, sort of like a soft and insistent howl, outside my open window.

Getting up, I blinked into the darkness.

"Hey," whispered Soup, "come on down."

Dressed in his clothes, he was standing under the apple tree that was close to our house. The front of Soup's shirt bulged with a strange-looking lump.

"No," I told Soup. "It's late."

Soup shrugged. "Suit yourself. But if you don't, we'll never win the goat race, come Saturday."

"We won't win as *laundry*."

"Well," said Soup, "there's always a chance. Ya want old Norma Jean Bissell to see us race, don't you?"

"Sort of. What time is it?"

"Real early. It's only ten o'clock. Or maybe eleven. So hurry up and climb down."

I sighed.

Why I climbed out of the window, in my pajamas, and then scraped myself down our apple tree, I'll never understand. Perhaps it was just one of those crazy things people do when they're half asleep. Or half nuts.

"What's up?" I asked Soup.

My pal grinned. "Practice," he said.

"*Huh?*"

"Hush," he whispered. "We gotta get away from your house, as well as mine, or we'll wake up everybody and catch holy hopscotch."

Sleepily, I followed Soup. Out beyond the barn we went, cutting through the cow pasture where I stepped into something that prompted a fresh regret that I was barefoot.

73

"Hurry," said Soup.

"Where to?"

He pointed at the rocks beyond our meadow. "Up there. To our cave."

It wasn't much of a cave, only big enough to accommodate Soup and me. The secret cave had served, in the past, as both a pirate's den and a cowboy's bunkhouse, as well as a gangster's hideout. But now, according to Soup, who was busy applying a lighted match to the stub of a white candle, the cave would fill one more mysterious purpose.

"You'll never guess what I found in our old piano bench," said Soup.

"No," I said. "I probable won't."

Pulling a wad of paper from inside his shirt, Soup unrolled it. He held it closer to the flickering light. "It's a sheet of music," he said. "So we can hold song practice."

"Here? In the cave?"

Soup nodded. "It's our last chance to really memorize the words and tune to the song."

I looked down at the sheet of music to read the song's title. Somehow, I already knew what it would be. Sure enough. "A Tropical Moon and You."

Quickly, my eye scanned the words:

> *I don't want a caribou.*
> *Just a fuzzy kinkajou,*
> *A parrot and a cockatoo,*
> *A tropical moon. And you.*

I don't want an ice igloo.
Just a hut of green bamboo,
A mango, and a honeydew,
A tropical moon. And you.

We'll . . .
Swim in murky lagoons.
Eat macaroons and prunes.
In spite of baboons, or a typhoon,
We'll still have the moon . . .
. . . over Rangoon.

I don't want no Mountain Dew.
Just a coconut shampoo,
And a peek at your tattoo . . .
A tropical moooooon.
And yooooo.

Even though I was still half asleep, I managed to say, "That's the song our class is learning to sing to Dr. Frank Sumatra when he comes for Goat Day."

"Right," said Soup, wearing a sly smile. "We want to really belt it out for Dr. Sumatra. And loud."

"Why do *we* have to practice it?"

"Because," said Soup, "we wanna make Goat Day a real corker of a success for Miss Boland. That's why."

"Then we're doing it for *her*."

"Well," said Soup, "in a way."

We sang.

Huddled together in the dark of our cave, Soup and I rehearsed "A Tropical Moon and You," singing even louder than the *bloops* of Miss Boland's tuba. But we probable sounded more like her Hoover. Not her car. Her vacuum cleaner.

Nonetheless, what Soup and I lacked in music talent, we made up for in volume. With the knobs on all four of our tonsils twisted up to high voltage, inside the cave our tenor notes really bounced around in the darkness. And once, on a high tone, our voices blew out the candle.

Quickly, we relit it.

We sang "A Tropical Moon and You" no less than seven hundred times. Or so it seemed.

Soup and I warbled in the cave until my eyelids sagged and my chin kept bumping down onto the shirt of my pajamas. The words we learned to perfection. The melody, however, took a beating. Gordon could have sung better than either one of us.

"One more time," insisted Soup.

"Never," I croaked back to him in a voice now thoroughly weakened from too many tropical moons. My throat felt as though I'd gargled with a mixture of gravel and broken glass.

I still couldn't fully understand Soup's sudden, and unexplained, interest in singing. At school, under the able baton (her ruler) of Miss Kelly, both of us sang about as well as a hacksaw calling to its mate. But knowing Soup, I had to presume there was a reason.

We blew out the candle. Then hid it. In the sky there was no moon. Not even a tropical one. The night had turned an inky black.

Soup and I practically had to feel our way, inch by inch, across the darkness of the cow pasture, toward my house. We were nearing a corner of our barn when it happened. My heart almost stopped when I suddenly heard a noise, and a second later saw a strange shape ahead of us. I was so scared I couldn't breathe.

Then a light quickly flashed into my eyes and into Soup's. Instinctively my hand shot upward to ward off the blinding glare.

"I'm telling on you two."

At first, possibly because of the piercing flashlight and the mysterious darkness, I didn't recognize the speaker. But then I did.

It was Sexton.

Eleven

"Soup," I said, "we're in trouble."

It was Thursday morning, so the two of us were naturally on our way to school.

"You owe me a nickel," Soup told me.

"A whole nickel! How come?"

"Because," said Soup as we walked down the dirt road, "I had to cough up a whole *dime* to pay Sexton for not squealing that we snuck out last night."

"I'm surprised all he wanted was a dime," I told Soup. "We got off cheap."

Soup looked at me with a sour face. "Yeah," he said, "only a dime—*per day.*"

I stopped. "You mean he'll want *another dime* tomorrow?"

"Check," said Soup. "And on Saturday, one more. Sexton Dilly gets a dime a day, or he snitches on both of us."

I kicked a pebble. It went sailing off the shoulder of the road and into a stand of cattails. "Golly," I said, "we'll both go flat-busted-broke in a week."

"Cheer up," said Soup. "With a bit of luck, I just

might be able to fit dear Cousin Sexton into my plan. It'll be duck soup."

"How?"

Soup shot me a wink. "Don't worry."

"Me?" I faked a hollow laugh. "I never worry. Certainly not over a little old thing like my folks finding out that we sneaked off at night. One word from Sexton Dilly, and both of our geese are cooked. I'll be ordered to stay in my room and miss all of Goat Day and so'll you."

My pal gave me an easy punch. "Rob, old tiger, there's one little fact of life that ya best learn and real sudden."

"What's that?"

"There's a place in the world for everybody," said Soup. "Even for Sexton. And," he added, his face easing into a smirk, "there's almost a place for Sexton in my Goat Day plan."

"Honest?"

Soup nodded.

I could see that he didn't seem to be too stewed or worried. Instead, he merely climbed up on a rail fence that ran along the road and walked the top rail, holding out his skinny arms for perfect balance. To me, his composure lay little short of a marvel.

Soup and I, although the two of us lived farther from the school than anyone else, were almost always the first ones there. On some mornings, we actually got to school ahead of even Miss Kelly. But on this particular morning, as we neared the little red-brick structure, I noticed that neither Soup nor I was first.

My heart leaped. Ahead I saw Norma Jean Bissell. She saw me coming and smiled.

Soup snickered. "Unless you're extra careful, old sport," he muttered to me, "you could wind up, a lot sooner than you think, saddled with a Mrs. Peck. And I don't mean your mother. Hear?"

I no longer heard.

Instead, my eyes strained forward, bulging from their sockets, eager for that first glimpse of her adorable dimple. Nostrils aflare, I even attempted, at a range of sixty feet, to inhale just one sweet wafting hint of her perfume. Both my heart and sneakers quickened, and my lips began to pucker.

"That's it," Soup told me. "Ignore her."

Girls, according to Luther Wesley Vinson, were nothing but trouble. A girl, as Soup usually saw her, was someone who would eventually interfere with freedom, baseball, or (in my case) normal blood circulation. Soup avoided girls, stepping around them wider than a cat around a puddle.

We came closer.

Soup grunted a "hi" to Norma Jean, flashed me a warning glare, and disappeared through the door and into the schoolhouse.

"Good morning, Rob."

The voice that purred was hers, Norma Jean's. Every word she spoke to me could strum my innards like a bow on a fiddle string. My heart clanged louder than a giant golden gong.

"Hi," I said.

"Isn't it a beautiful day?"

The tinkle of her voice played upon my spine as though I had become a xylophone. But the feeling seemed mainly to center in the pit of my stomach, as if my navel had sprouted wings. Or lint.

"Yup," I said, having so acutely perfected my art of courtship and conversation.

"I hope you win on Saturday," said Norma Jean, in tones that sped the flow of my juices into a rate that would humble a comet.

"Thanks," I said, again impressing her with my agility of quick retort.

A week or so earlier, I had, in a moment of weakness, confessed to Soup that it might be a dandy idea if, just once, I walked home from school with Norma Jean Bissell. My suggestion had then prompted Soup to emit a very disgusting noise.

"*Yuk!*" he had gagged.

That's why I was so doggone surprised to see Soup coming back out of the schoolhouse. Even more amazed when Soup looked at Norma Jean Bissell with a friendly smile.

"Norma Jean," I heard Soup say, "I got an idea. I think old Robert here ought to walk home from school with *you* sometime soon. If you don't mind."

Norma Jean's eyes brightened with enthusiasm. So did mine. And yet, there was a certain tone in Soup's voice that I could only interpret with total mistrust. He, I was thinking, was up to something, and I'd wager that it had little to do with my being with Norma Jean, or she with me.

One glance at Norma Jean's face informed me, as she eyed Soup, that she was thinking the same thing. Her hands rested on her hips. "Okay, Luther Vinson, what's the catch?"

No fool she, I thought.

Soup shrugged. "Well," he said, "to be perfectly honest about it, Norma Jean, I'd sort of like to ask if you'd do us a favor."

"So I figured," she said.

My pal shifted his weight from one foot to the other, perhaps realizing that he now faced brains as well as beauty. But then he turned to me.

"Rob, be a good guy and let me speak, in private, to Norma Jean."

"Why?" I asked.

"It's a surprise," he said. "For you, old top."

"Honest?"

"Yup."

"Okay," I said. Then, before I dashed into the front door of the schoolhouse, I looked at my girl. A pang of panic suddenly hit me. Was good old Soup planning to move in and take Norma Jean Bissell away from me forever? "Hey," I said to Soup, *"you're* not fixing to walk home with her, are ya?"

The relieving answer came quicker than expected, as Norma Jean looked at Soup.

"Yuk!" she said.

Twelve

"Ready?" yelled Miss Boland.

Goat Day had arrived. There we were, all lined up in our goat carts at the starting line. Soup and I were standing inside *DIRTY LAUNDRY,* which had no seat, trying to keep our balance.

I was looking around to see if I could spot Norma Jean Bissell. Oddly, she seemed not to be in the crowd. Our town was packed with people of all ages, including our famous visitor, Dr. Frank Sumatra.

Miss Boland, wearing her pith helmet, carrying her tuba, and leading Gordon on a leash, stood beside Dr. Sumatra. He was sure a tiny little man. Not much bigger than Gordon. Nonetheless, it was plain to see that Miss Boland appeared to be totally entranced in the company of our distinguished guest.

"The race," she hollered to the crowd, "is now about to begin. And our celebrated visitor, Dr. Frank Sumatra, will personally award the prize to the winner."

I stole a glance at Janice Riker, whose burly fists held a whip and Geronimo's reins. Her cart, *CHARGER*, looked to be the fastest cart.

Next to her, Ally Tidwell waited in the smallest cart. *HUSTLER* was painted on its side in bright blue. His goat, Winthrop, looked sleeker and faster than Geronimo.

Eddy Tacker, in a super-looking cart named *TORNADO*, looked more than eager to urge Hector, his goat, to a victory. Of the four goat carts, *DIRTY LAUNDRY*, with regard to appearance, came in a dismal fourth. If it came in at all.

"Soup," I said, "look at *their* carts compared to ours. We're driving a junk heap."

"Don't worry," Soup told me. "Janice, Ally, and Eddy may have the sharpest carts. But we've got the smartest *plan.*"

Soup's secret with Norma Jean Bissell was still pestering me a mite. "Say," I asked him, "what *favor* did you ask of Norma Jean?"

"It's a surprise," he said. "And it doesn't have anything to do with a duck."

In the crowd, I spotted Mama, Papa, and Aunt Carrie. They waved, and I waved too. With them stood Soup's parents, along with Aunt Louise and Uncle

Bunker. I looked for good old Sexton but couldn't see him. Maybe because he was too short.

"Ready?" Miss Boland asked us again.

"Hold it," yelled Janice Riker. "It ain't fair." She pointed her whip at Soup and me. "Them two guys only got one cart."

"It's fair," Soup said to Miss Boland, "because Janice grabbed all the construction material. Or most of it."

Our nurse eyed the carts, one by one. As she examined our sloppy old wagon, she almost winced.

"No," said Miss Boland, "it's not fair. Nobody," she added, nodding at our cart, "should risk life and limb in *that.*"

Soup grinned. "It's all for fun," he said.

Miss Boland smiled at us. "Right," she said, "so let's get this goat race on the road. Now don't forget the route, you kids. Up through town by the Baptist church, across the bridge, and around Mr. Dooley's barn. Then you go past the Methodist Church, cross lots to the feed store, go by the big oak tree, then down the home stretch and to the finish line. Right here."

"Okay," said Soup.

"And don't forget, folks," Miss Boland told the crowd, "after the race, we'll honor Dr. Sumatra with a song. And," she added with a shy smile, "a tuba solo."

Dr. Frank Sumatra appeared as though he longed to be back exploring the South Seas. Or someplace where Miss Boland wouldn't be blooping her tuba.

"All racers ready?"

High in the air, Miss Boland held her cap pistol. My stomach felt as if the race would never start and my indigestion would never end.

"On your marks!" Miss Boland warned. "Get set! And . . ."

Her cap pistol misfired. *"Blaaa,"* bleated Gordon. Yet, keeping calm, Miss Boland didn't give up. "Get set," she then repeated, grabbing her tuba, "and . . ."

Bloop!

We were off! The great race of Goat Day was on. Geronimo, Hector, and Winthrop all charged, followed by swift carts.

"Soup," I said with alarm. "We're not racing."

Orbit and Nesbit, hitched side by side, merely trotted forward in leisure as Janice, Ally, and Eddy pulled ahead of us at full gallop.

I poked Soup in the ribs. "Didn't you hear?" I was hollering at him. "The race has started! Even though Miss Boland's cap pistol didn't fire."

No sooner had I spoken my final word—*fire*—I thought my neck was broken. Orbit and Nesbit exploded forward faster than twin bullets.

"Hang on, Rob," yelled Soup. "You've got the reins, haven't ya?"

"No," I hollered. "I thought you had 'em."

All I could see was sky, as Soup and I were tumbling around in the bottom of our *DIRTY LAUN-DRY* basket in an effort to grab anything. Including each other. Finally, we staggered to our feet as a *blur* seemed to go by, in the opposite direction.

"What," I asked Soup, "was *that?*"

"It looked like the Baptist Church," Soup answered, "but I ain't too blessed sure."

Up ahead, *CHARGER* and *HUSTLER* and *TOR-NADO* roared on. But we were rapidly closing the gap. Then we sped by all three carts as though they were parked. We were in the *lead!*

"Find the reins," Soup yelled. "Because I think we're coming to the bridge."

My hand felt an old length of rope. "I got one," I said. "I think it's Nesbit's."

"Great," said Soup. "I got hold of something too. And I sure hope it's Orbit's."

"No," I said as we tumbled down into the bottom of the basket again, "that's my belt. Let go."

Too late! I heard a *snap* and then, as I tried to stand up, I felt my pants starting to slip. Soup, who was still down, was trying to climb up my right leg. Trouble was, as Soup moved up, my pants moved down.

Standing at last, I felt a sudden breeze whistling through my adult-selected underwear. My trouseres, however, fell to my ankles like a defeated flag.

"We've got to slow down, Soup," I said. "So I can pull up my pants."

Soup, however, was now far more in the spirit of racing than he was for my dressing.

"Go, Orbit, go!" he cried.

"Whoa, Nesbit, whoa," I pleaded.

We hit a big bump.

How our cart, *DIRTY LAUNDRY*, ever sailed over the bridge at a height of ten feet, I'll never know. Orbit and Nesbit must have touched the bridge with their hoofs. Our wheels didn't. But at least, as I soared on high, I had a chance to yank up my pants.

Flying through the air, Soup and I then learned, was one thing. Landing, however, was quite another.

Over we spilled. Soup, fortunately for him, was unhurt in the crash. It's easier when you have a pal, like me, to land on. As I hit Vermont, Soup hit me. Opening my eyes, all I could see was our cart. It was upside down in the middle of the road. Its four wheels still spun crazily, around and around, going nowhere. All I could read was the letters:

DIRTY LAUNDRY

Where, I wondered, were our goats?

"Nesbit," I called.

"Orbit," called Soup.

"*Blaa! Blaaa!*" came two muffled answers.

"Come on, Rob," said Soup, as he got off me. "Our goats are under the cart. Inside."

Over we tipped it. Out they came. Luckily, as we righted our vehicle, the goats waited for Soup and me to climb aboard *DIRTY LAUNDRY*.

"*Hyah!*" said Soup.

Forward they trotted. Yet something was now

missing. It was speed. Orbit and Nesbit were no longer in a mood to run. All they did was trot. Worse yet, as we got to Mr. Dooley's barn, Janice passed us. So did Alley and Eddy.

"*Now!*" yelled Soup. But he didn't yell his one-word command to Orbit or to Nesbit. Not even to me. He yelled it at Mr. Dooley's barn.

That's when I got the surprise of my life. From inside the barn, out came about a dozen girls. In the lead was Norma Jean Bissell. Each girl had a cheerleader megaphone, and all of them began to sing almost as loud as a public address system.

They sang "A Tropical Moon and You."

Soup sang too. And so did I. For a moment, it seemed as though the entire world was blasting out "A Tropical Moon and You," the song that the band had played on the night of the circus fire.

Our goats almost flew in sheer panic.

Inch by inch, we gained ground on Eddy's Hector, Ally's Winthrop, and finally on Janice's Geronimo.

Soup punched me. "Sing," he was yelling. "Sing the doggone song as loud as you can. Louder than a circus band in a fire."

I really sang.

Thirteen

All five goats raced neck and neck.

Close behind came all four goat carts and the five contestants—Janice in *CHARGER*, Ally in *HUSTLER*, Eddy in *TORNADO*, and Soup and me tumbling around in *DIRTY LAUNDRY*.

We whizzed by the Methodist Church so fast that it appeared only to be a ghostly blurr.

Soup and I kept singing "A Tropical Moon and You" as loud as we possibly could. But it wasn't loud enough. Our voices didn't seem to be convincing either Orbit or Nesbit. The other three carts were pulling ahead of us as we tore past the feed store.

Dead ahead stood the largest and oldest oak tree in the town of Learning.

"This is it," said Soup. "Here's our secret weapon."

Our cart, now rattling behind and hopelessly trailing all the others, took the turn really wide. Ahead, a long overhanging limb stretched out, almost blocking our path. Sitting on the big limb was somebody. But, as we were bouncing around so badly, I couldn't make out who it was. I was hoping it was a doctor.

A second or two later, I found out.

"Jump!" yelled Soup.

Whoever it was, jumped. The jumper landed on my back and held on, with hands covering my eyes.

"Now," said Soup. "Do your stuff *or else.*"

Before I could ask Soup what was going on, who our third passenger was, and exactly what *stuff* the person was supposed to do, I heard . . .

"KZTYPTD QMP XP TLDPRZ XWKL PDBCF FFT SHLTY DMPN RTFBG HZT KX JPMWXKGZ PDG."

Our third rider had to be either Donald Duck or Sexton Dilly.

I couldn't believe what I was hearing. But, up in front, Orbit and Nesbit certainly heard. And believed! You'll never see two goats spook away from a duck any faster than those two goats.

"Louder," yelled Soup to Sexton. "Quack louder, or Rob and I'll rat to your folks all about your swearing, and you'll be in trouble for the rest of your life."

As we flew down the home stretch, passing the other carts toward the finish line and a cheering crowd, several things happened:

Sexton swore like Donald Duck, Soup sang "A Tropical Moon and You," Orbit and Nesbit ran faster and faster until the harness broke, a wheel came off our baby carriage, and my pants fell down again.

"Lean," hollered Soup.

We leaned, all three of us. Our loose wheel, Orbit, and Nesbit sped ahead without us. How trusty old *DIRTY LAUNDRY* ever managed to zip over the finish line first, *on three wheels*, I will never know.

I was hoping that *DIRTY LAUNDRY* would then coast to a graceful stop, but no such luck. That cart seemed to have a mind of its own.

"Soup," I yelped, "we're headed right at Miss Boland and Dr. Frank Sumatra."

"Not to mention," said Sexton, "the refreshment stand."

Women screamed. Strong men fainted. Yet on we flew, now goatless and on three wheels, toward an unavoidable collision. Closing my eyes, I prayed for a quick and painless death.

We crashed!

High into the Vermont air flew cake, ice cream, hot dogs, gobs of mustard, a tuba, a pith helmet, Gordon, and Sexton Dilly, along with Soup, me, and *DIRTY LAUNDRY*. It took several seconds for everything, and everyone, to fly, land, and roll to a dead stop.

Soup groaned. So did I.

Sexton, however, said absolutely nothing, clean or dirty, because it isn't very easy to talk, sing, or swear when you're lying beneath Miss Boland. Sexton's head was inside the giant bell of her tuba.

Slowly, painfully, we all unpiled.

"We won, Rob," said Soup. "I can't wait to see what the prize is."

"I hope," I told him, "that it's a free trip, all expenses paid, to the hospital."

I ached all over. Even my freckles were yelping in pain. Yet the joy of our victory, especially over Janice Riker, slowly began to brighten my spirits. To make me even happier, I saw Sexton, who was completely dirty.

As the air finally cleared, Miss Boland asked Dr. Frank Sumatra to award the prize. He then presented Soup and me with our reward. The prize was Gordon!

But then came an even bigger surprise.

"Congratulations," said Sexton as he shook my hand and Soup's. "And thanks to both of you guys, I'm completely cured."

"Cured?" I asked.

"Yes," he said. "I'll never swear again."

"Good," I told him. "You're okay, Sexton. Without you, Soup and I would never have won the goat race."

Soup clapped his cousin on the back. "Rob's right, Sexton. You're really an okay kid. You're even dirty."

"Gee thanks," he told us, smiling.

Then I saw Sexton's mother, Aunt Louise, storming our way. Uncle Bunker was trailing behind her. Eyes aflame, she pointed at her son and his filthy clothes.

"I swear," she shrieked.

Soup shot me a wink. "Well," he said, "I guess it just runs in the family."

Everybody crowded around Soup and me to congratulate us on winning. Yet we both made sure to thank Miss Kelly, Dr. Frank Sumatra, Miss Boland, Mr. Arno Fletcher, and Norma Jean Bissell.

But then Soup and I started arguing as to which one of us would keep Gordon. We couldn't very easily divide a tiny goat in half. The solution came to both of us. Soup and I knew the perfect happy ending.

We gave Gordon to Sexton, for keeps.

ROBERT NEWTON PECK writes from experience, and he's had a lot of it. He has been a soldier, a lumberjack, a football player and a hog butcher. He claims, though, that he is a farmer at heart and his favorite stories are about his own boyhood in rural Vermont.

A prolific author, he has written 36 books including the highly acclaimed *A Day No Pigs Would Die* and *Soup For President,* winner of the Mark Twain Award.

Mr. Peck lives with his family in Longwood, Florida, but he's often on the road, traveling to schools and colleges to talk about writing and books.